the Stone-cutter

a Japanese folk tale

adapted & illustrated by
Gerald McDermott

THE VIKING PRESS   NEW YORK

FOR MY MOTHER

The author wishes to thank Sidney Forman
for his contribution to the original script
of the film The Stonecutter.

ABOUT THE ARTIST

GERALD MCDERMOTT has created both
animated films and illustrated books. His
graphic interpretation of mythology in these
media has brought him numerous
international awards; in 1975 he received
the Caldecott Award for his book Arrow
to the Sun.

ABOUT THE BOOK

To prepare the art for this book, the artist
hand-colored large sheets of white bond paper
with gouache. He then cut out his design
forms and mounted them as collages. The art
was reproduced in four-color process. The
text type is Koronna Bold; the display is Serif
Gothic Extra Bold. The book was printed on
an 80-pound white vellum stock by offset and
is bound in cloth over boards. The binding
is reinforced and side-sewn.

First published in 1975 by The Viking Press, Inc.
625 Madison Avenue, New York, N.Y. 10022
Distributed in Canada by
Penguin Books Canada Limited

PRINTED IN U.S.A.

2   3   4   5   79

Library of Congress Cataloging
in Publication Data
McDermott, Gerald. The stonecutter.
[1. Folklore—Japan]   I. Title.
PZ8.1.M159St   398.2'2'0952   [E] 74—26823

ISBN 0—670—67074—x

the Stone-cutter

Tasaku was a lowly stonecutter. Each day the sound of his hammer and chisel rang out as he chipped away at the foot of the mountain. He hewed the blocks of stone that formed the great temples and palaces.

He asked for nothing more
than to work each day,
and this pleased the spirit
who lived in the mountains.

One day, a prince went
by. Soldiers preceded him,
musicians and dancers
followed him. He was
clothed in beautiful silk
robes, and his servants
carried him aloft.
Tasaku watched until
the magnificent procession
had passed out of sight.

Tasaku cut no more stone
and returned to his hut.
He envied the prince. He
looked up into the sky and
wished aloud that he might
have such great wealth.
Then he slept.

The spirit who lived in
the mountains heard him...

and that night
transformed the
stonecutter into
a prince.

Tasaku was overjoyed.
He lived in a palace and
wore robes of the finest silk.
Musicians played for him
and servants bowed low.
He commanded great armies
and ruled over the land.

Every afternoon Tasaku
walked in his garden.
He loved the fragrant
petals and graceful vines.
But the sun burned his
flowers. He knelt over
the withered blossoms
and saw the power of
the sun.

Tasaku wanted to be as
powerful, so he asked the
spirit who lived in the
mountains to change him
into the sun.

The spirit heard him.

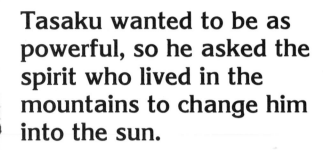

Tasaku became the sun,
and he was happy
for a time.
To show his power he
burned the fields and
parched the lands.
The people begged
for water.

Then a cloud came and
covered him, and the
bright rays of the sun
were obscured. Tasaku
then knew the cloud
was even more powerful
than the sun. He told
the spirit to change him
into a cloud.

The spirit heard him.

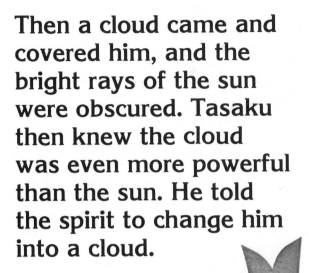

Tasaku became the cloud.
With his new power he made
violent storms. Thunder
rolled across the sky,
rivers overran their banks,
fields were flooded, huts
and palaces were washed
away.

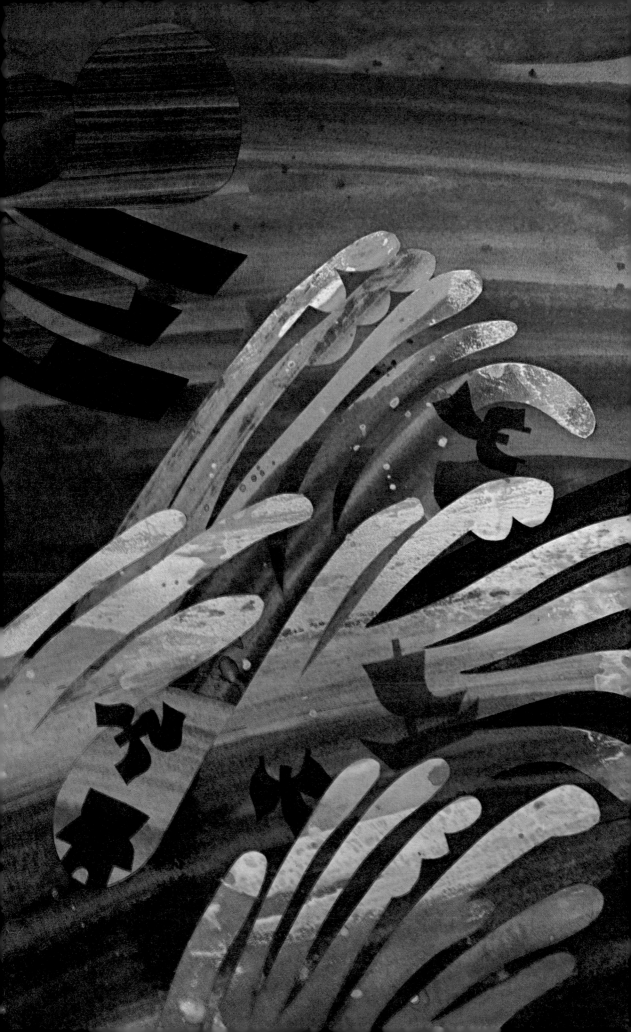

But the mountain remained.

Tasaku was angry because
the mountain was more
powerful than the cloud.
"Make me into the mountain!"
Tasaku demanded. The
spirit obeyed and then
departed, for there was
nothing more he could do.

Tasaku became the mountain. He was more powerful than the prince, stronger than the sun, mightier than the cloud.

But Tasaku felt the sharp
sting of a chisel. It was a
lowly stonecutter, chipping
away at his feet.

Deep inside, he trembled.